I0712765

HALEY GOT A HAT-TRICK

Written by **Lexie Demko** • Illustrated by **Kiandokht Khalili**

Haley woke up on Saturday and rolled out of bed.

She pulled on her jersey and down the stairs she sped.

She grabbed a bagel and orange juice and turned on the TV.

She flipped right to the hockey highlights so exciting to see...

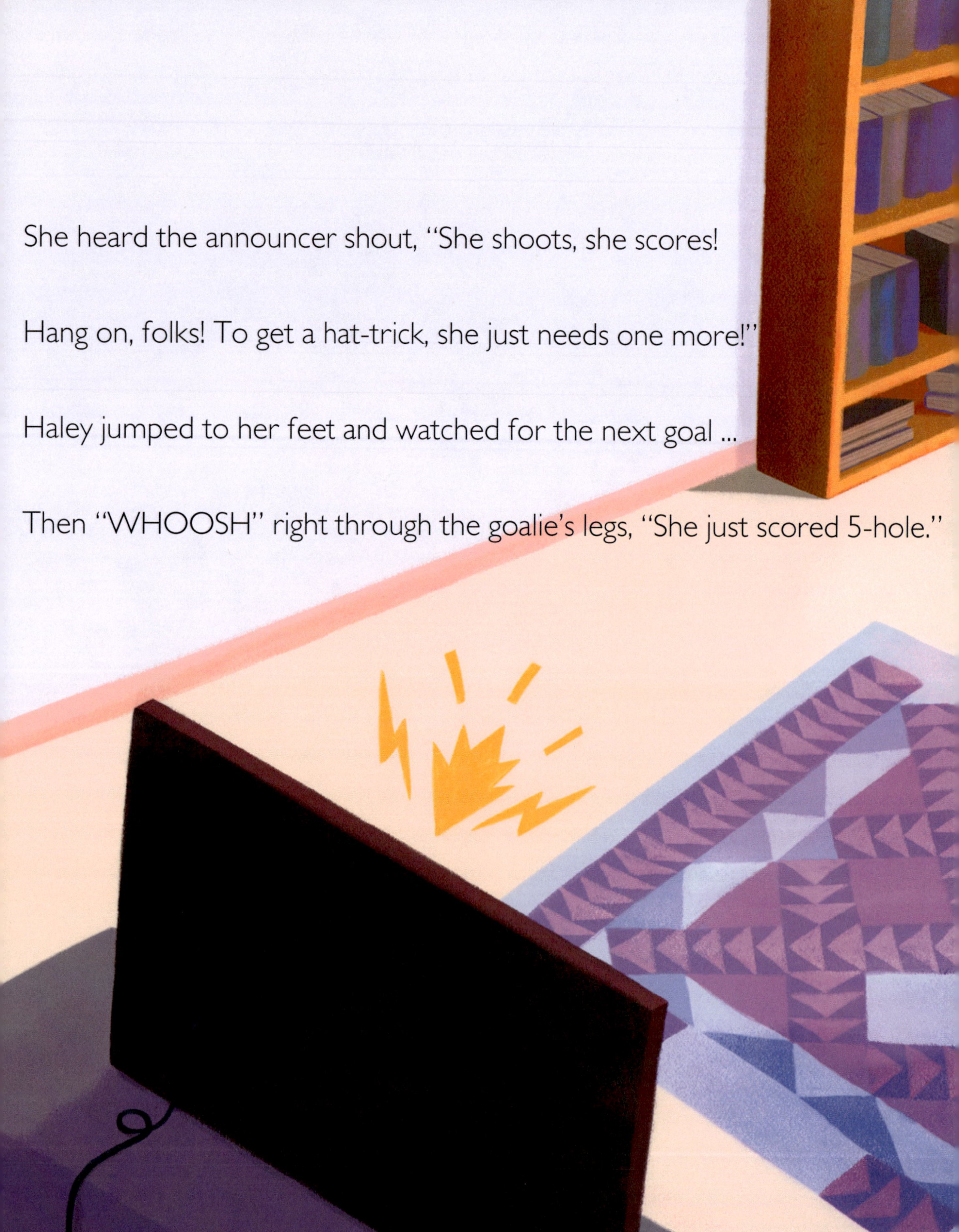

She heard the announcer shout, "She shoots, she scores!

Hang on, folks! To get a hat-trick, she just needs one more!"

Haley jumped to her feet and watched for the next goal ...

Then "WHOOSH" right through the goalie's legs, "She just scored 5-hole."

Haley stared at the screen, admiring the words in bold

"THREE GOALS GETS A HAT-TRICK - GOING FOR GOLD!"

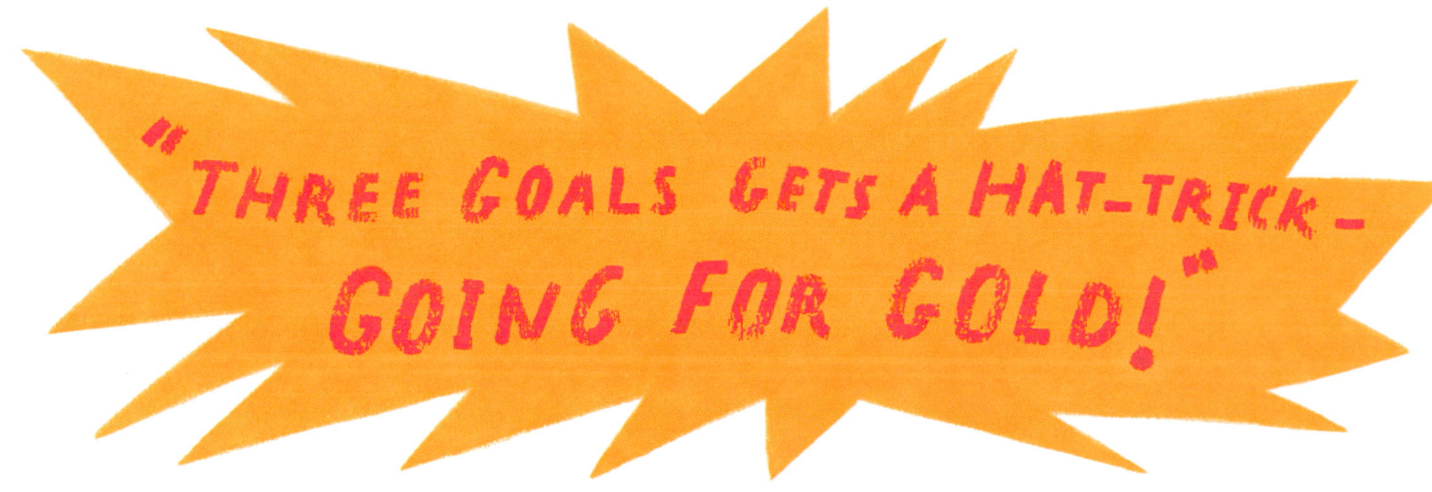

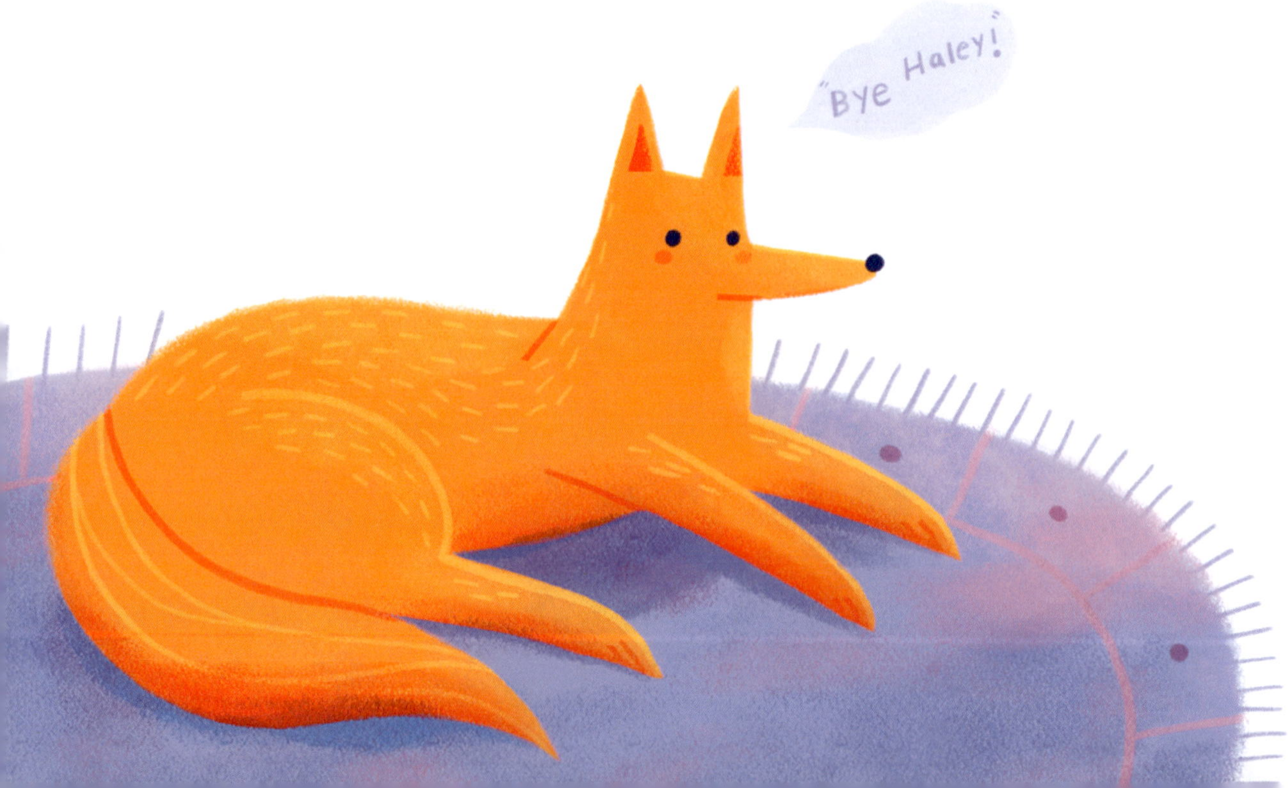

"Time to go," her mom announced, "You really need to hurry."

Haley grabbed her hockey bag and packed it in a flurry.

H·A·L·E·Y
7

In the car, Haley thought, "Today will be my day!"

"I'll strive for a hat-trick, too, three goals when I play!"

With success set in mind, she put her gear on quick,

The last important thing to do was to retape her stick.

"This fresh tape will help me get the three goals that I need!

I'll also need my bullseye shots, dekes and super speed!"

After warm-ups finished, the buzzer sounded for puck drop.

Three forwards, two defensemen and one goalie to stop.

Haley raced to battle and she won the puck,

She took a shot, but she missed ... She whispered, "Just bad luck."

During her turn on the bench, she thought up a plan …

"I'll keep the puck to myself as much as I possibly can!"

Her next shift on the ice, she knew she had to score.

Her teammate passed her the puck and she shot from back door.

GOAL! Haley scored, and she heard the fans roar.

She whispered again, "One goal down … I just need two more!"

Two periods go by, now it's the start of the third,

Haley's coach pulled her aside ... "We need to have a word."

"You're skating hard, you're looking strong and doing great out there,

But next time when you get the puck, maybe you should share!"

Haley looked up at her coach, then swirled around her stick.

"But if I share the puck," she said, "I won't get my Hat-Trick!"

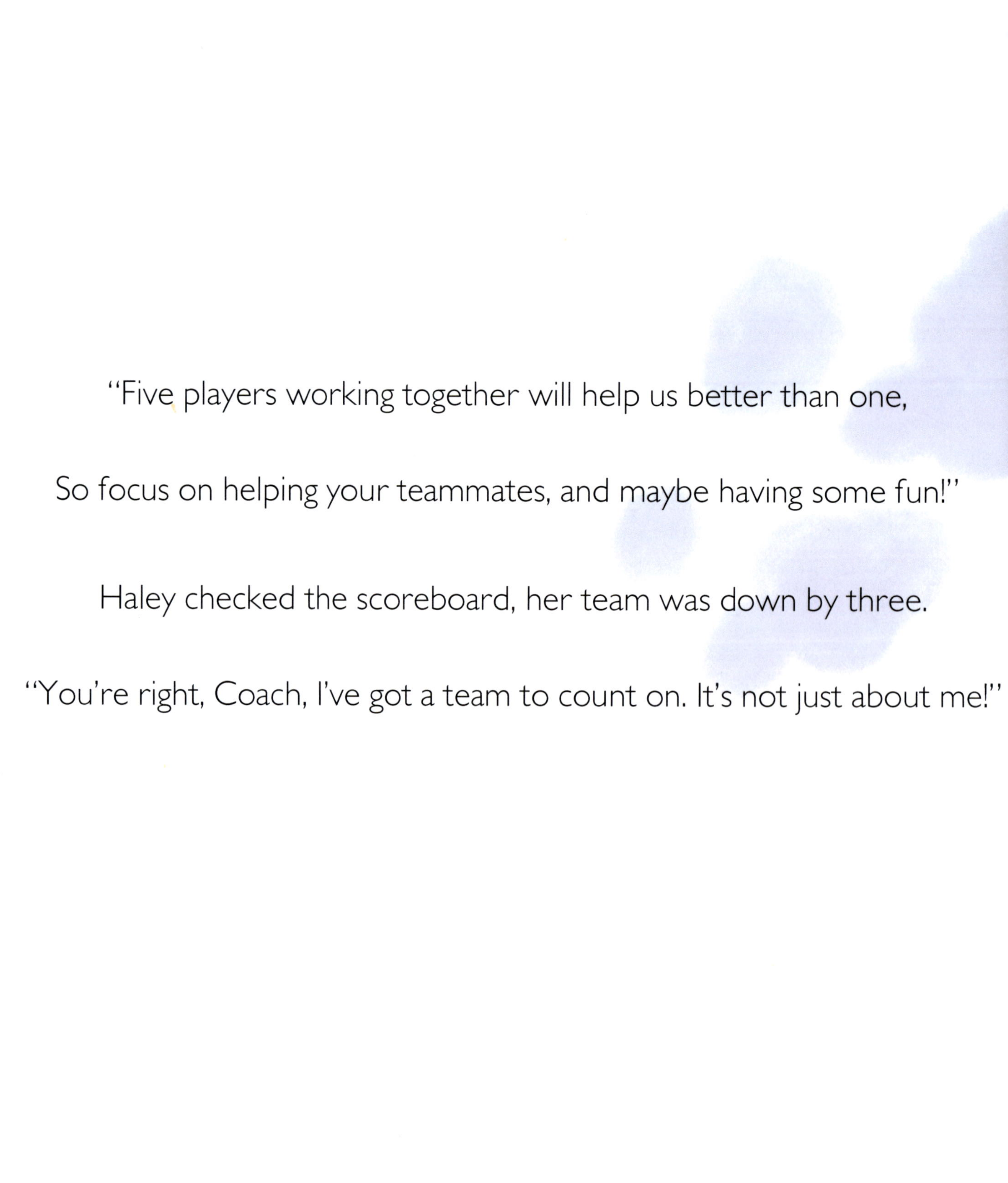

"Five players working together will help us better than one,

So focus on helping your teammates, and maybe having some fun!"

Haley checked the scoreboard, her team was down by three.

"You're right, Coach, I've got a team to count on. It's not just about me!"

Haley took the face-off and saw an open teammate.

Right away, she passed the puck and then started to skate.

Haley headed to the net as her teammate had control ...

He threw the puck at the net and she tipped in her second goal!

"Good job, team!" Haley huddled up, and the players' hopes all grew.

The numbers on the scoreboard moved ... now it read 4 – 2.

As Haley watched from the bench, another teammate scored!

It was now 4 – 3 ... they just needed one more!

Haley stepped out on the ice and skated towards the play,

She found the puck and passed it to the forward ... Then he had a breakawa

Her teammate deked to the left and then faked to the right,

The puck slammed into the net ...

FLICK! on went the goal light.

"Thanks for the perfect pass, Haley!" and they shared a high five,

"Do you believe it? Two minutes left, finally we are tied!"

Now it was 4 - 4 and Haley's last shift of the game.

She had a hold of the puck, then she heard someone call her name.

The forward was wide open again, and he had a clear shot ...

Haley tossed him the puck and skated right to the slot.

Her teammate took a hard slap shot ... a "DING!" pinged from the net,

Did it go in? "Yes!" Haley thought, but the goal light was not on yet!

"REBOUND!" Coach yelled from the bench, as he pointed to the puck.

It was right in front of Haley, so she wound up and struck!

The puck zoomed passed the goalie and the fans started to cheer!

"We won! We won!"

Her teammates chant was all Haley could hear.

Coach said, "Way to play hard out there and come together as a team

When every player works together on the ice, that's when we succeed!"

Coach patted Haley on the back and gave her a huge grin.

"You were awesome, today, Haley, and a big part of this win!"

He handed her the puck and said, "Your three goals wowed the crowd.

Haley got her Hat Trick! And she was VERY proud!

www.ingramcontent.com/pod-product-compliance
Lightning Source LLC
Chambersburg PA
CBRC101119300726
48981CB00013B/475